THE PARKER CHRONICLES

Glimpses of observed suburban lives

R.A. Cramblitt

BC Publishing Inc.

ISBN: 978-0-578-93978-0

Taming the brute

Parker knew that if he didn't read stuff that engaged his mind at another level, if he didn't take time to look at art or listen to or play music, take time to walk and think, he would be an emotional brute. It happened too many times, especially when he thought the world was bending in tune with his needs and desires. The attendant regrets from those times make him flinch and redden in shame. He knows he isn't alone. There are many in his company, and many more without his bred-in compunction.

The lying shrink

Jim Cain's practice was in a strip office complex a stone's throw from Rt. 55. He shared the reception area with an accountant, an IT consultant and a math tutor. Parker could never tell the psychiatric patients from the more prosaic clients. He picked up a nine-month old, oversized and graphics-studded issue of *ESPN the Magazine* and started reading about Dwayne Wade's fashion sensibilities.

A slouching kid and his brisk mother walked by. Cain peeked in the lobby a minute later and called for Parker to follow. Cain's a chronic liar. Or maybe not. He once told Parker he saw the game where Wilt scored 100 in 1962 in Hershey, Pennsylvania. Cain was from New England and would have been about 14 at the time. Attendance was 4,124.

Parker wasn't sure if Cain was testing him; wanting him to assert himself and call Cain a liar or if he just liked mythology. Parker still doesn't know.

You could be an asshole

Parker was recounting his weekend to Cain, his therapist.

"Shelly and I got into it again. We were drinking, she more heavily than me, and she went from laughing and hugging me to berating me."

"Over what"?

"It starts with a seemingly benign question: 'Did it ever occur to you to help me out around the house once in a while'? I pointed out that I do a lot in addition to my full-time job: I do all the grocery shopping, yard work and help out sometimes with vacuuming. But my reply sounded pretty weak-ass even to me."

"She says, 'Oh, you're a regular Sebastian Cabot', you know, referring to the Mr. French man-servant character in that old TV series, *Family Affair*. She says 'You get all put out when I ask you to go shopping for stuff we need around the house.' I reply that I'm always willing to go shopping with her, but by now I'm cringing at my plaintive voice."

"'But why do I always have to bring it up several times before you agree to do it,' she says, her voice getting higher and louder. 'It's all about you, Will. All about you and your business. I'm like a servant to you. You don't give a shit about me.'

"I'm pounding the hassock now, screaming 'I do give a shit! I give several shits. I love you. You're the number one thing in my life.'

"I'm getting pissed off now, because I think this is totally unfair. She's taken this from zero to 60 in a matter of seconds.

"She says, 'You have a great way of showing it, Will. I'm not sure I can go into the future with you.'

"'Jesus, we were just having a great time, laughing and kissing, now this. You're killing me...why don't you just grab a knife'?

"'Oh, poor sensitive man. You know what? Screw this, I'm outta here; you're on your own,' she says, and stomps out of the room into the bedroom, slamming the door behind her. I'm fuming to the point of helplessness. One thing she's right about: I am sensitive, especially when I'm accused of not caring for her."

Cain leans back, fingers laced behind his neck. "Well, the self-perception of sensitivity can be a facet of selfishness. I was going on one time to my AA sponsor about how sensitive I am, how I feel things more than other people. He tells me, "Or you could just be an asshole.""

Will's willpower

Parker was no longer manageable in the traditional business sense of bowing to a so-called superior. He chafed under the bit. Unfortunately, when one's practice involves marketing and PR, the experts are legion -- basically anyone who has ever watched a commercial, read a best-selling marketing book or visited a web site. These people had frequent revelations, typically on airplanes, that they were anxious to share with Parker. He needed to smile. Be positive. Avoid any comments that smacked of "Jane you ignorant slut." Sometimes it took every ounce of his willpower.

The singer snob

In case he ever needed acknowledgement, Shelly gave it to him: "You're a singer snob."

Parker had just commented about the front woman's apparent need to show her entire voice range within a single bar.

"It was just like when we were in that restaurant and you started a treatise about that poor girl's singing after a few people commented innocently enough that she had a good voice."

"I didn't think she should be encouraged to sing in public until she learns something about time, melody and singing in a pitch that complements the musical accompaniment. Not much to ask for an alleged entertainer."

"But people were enjoying her."

"And some people enjoyed Jim Nabors' singing."

"Oh, jeez, not the Jim Nabors comparison."

"OK, then, maybe Mariah Carey ruining that Christmas song I used to like."

"You have a choice. Simply. Don't. Listen."

"No, I don't have a choice -- they're everywhere and there's no escape. Besides I'm no exhibitionist. I refuse to call attention to myself by clamping my hands over my ears."

"I'm rethinking being seen in public with you."

Failing the screen test

Parker snapped to attention from near sleep. He was half-consciously recalling an episode from college. Three decades later and regrets still clung to him like barnacles below a boat's water line.

He was at Bar None trying to get the attention of a girl he'd seen walking across campus. She was his type. Almost all were his type.

Her friend, a synapse-numbing blond who looked as if she stepped out of bed knock-them-dead gorgeous came over and sat across from him.

"So, you like Jennifer"?

"I don't know exactly. I've seen her around and like the way she walks. But I've never really spoken to her so I don't know if I'd like her or not. I'd like to talk to her, preferably alone. Are you screening me"?

"I wouldn't say that, but I'm her friend. She's been hurt before and I don't want to see it happen again. She's a great person and she deserves someone who really cares about her."

"Well, I've been with a lot of women..." Her eyes rolled -- the first time he'd ever seen that in a real situation. Tilt. Game over.

It's called privilege

Parker knew how lucky he was. He'd been called good-looking. He'd played basketball and had fans call his name. He'd won professional awards. He'd shared romping, sweaty, mutually joyous sex. He'd hung out with really cool people. He'd had moments of soaring, natural ecstasy. He'd had people who wanted to be near him; who wanted to be like him. He'd known, and still knows, nearly unconditional love.

He had great parents and siblings. The best cousins. Went to good schools and found the work relatively easy. He had little problem finding good jobs doing non-debilitating work. He'd aged well. There were a few bumps in his life, but nothing that registered on any level of the emotional Richter scale.

Sure, he did some things to earn his good fortune. But most of it came from riding the great hand he'd been dealt from birth. He'd gotten where he is by basically not fucking up. So his question, which he posed continually in response to people denigrating entire classes of people they don't understand as being lazy, immoral, criminal and leaches on the good graces of society, was simple: "Do you realize how lucky you are and that practically all of it comes down to luck of the draw at birth"?

Gym creatures in captivity

Two to three times a week, in between swimming and walking days, Parker goes to the gym. It's a small place, just machines, treadmills, ellipticals and free weights. Smaller is good for him -- less germ potential.

He likes the machines, the Nautilus, Cybex, Matrix things. Purists say you should always be supporting your weight when working out, but Parker loves a smooth-gliding weight machine.

He enters the 24/7 facility and greets the woman at the desk. She's the size of a pixie, but a pixie who could fling you across the room without spilling her smoothie. She's always looking at the computer screen. Looks up to give a perfunctory nod, then returns her rapt attention to what? Minute-by-minute statistics on who is doing what kind of exercise anywhere around the world?

There's that Ken-type guy with the coiffed, stationary hair. He has the coveted V-man taper and strains not to look at himself in the mirror after every rep.

There's the 20-something woman who played softball in college, blew out a knee, and is trying desperately to control the spread, the inexorable spread.

There's the grunter, although club guidelines printed in large type on the wall next to the mirror discourages it. He sometimes flips a tractor tire up and down the aisle, not only grunting, but causing a blunted exploding sound when the tire thuds to the floor -- another supposed no no.

There's the Anglo-Asian woman with perfect skin and a butt you could bounce a quarter off of and get two dimes and a nickel in change. She does about five sets of pelvic and leg lift exercises each session. Everybody looks at her while trying to look as if they aren't looking at her.

Oh, and the dreaded lurker. He'll do a set of five on the Matrix, then spend three minutes checking his phone. Another five, another three on the phone. Repeat twice. Parker has decided to giggle at this guy instead of seething. It's mentally healthier, and feels curiously righteous.

Quitting as a lifestyle

Quitters don't win and winners don't quit. Or something like that. Whatever it is Parker doesn't believe it.

One of his favorite all-time LPs, both in title and content, is "Born to Quit" by The Smoking Popes. The Popes sound like Dean Martin crooning over X-like west coast punk. They remind Parker that there is beauty and power in quitting, especially when you're facing recriminations real and imagined that shake your core.

Sure, he's heard people say, "You quit and he wins" or "I never took you for a quitter". Those comments made his skin prick. But then an indignity raises its hand in his mind like an eager school kid crying "ooo, ooo, ooo" and his nerves tingle.

Quitting didn't always lead to better things, but it made sense when faced with too many consecutive nights of bolting awake with the early morning sweats. Call him a coward and he might agree. But as a strategy, it worked for Parker.

If he was a more passionate guy and didn't mind volunteering for pain, Parker might even consider having "Born to Quit" emblazoned on his left bicep, just above "Shelly" in script within a faux-3D blood-red heart.

Honing chops at Peking Pancho

"Give me that knife before you hurt yourself and/or others," Parker says to his friend Ricky. They'd known each other since high school and along with seven other classmates were staging a reunion in Ocean City, Maryland.

"It's literally a dull knife that just ain't cuttin'," says Ricky.

"When it comes to choppin', you're not the sharpest knife in the drawer, brohammer."

While no professional, Parker knew a bit about prep work. He knew a lot about restaurant work, without having done much of it since he was a teenager. But, he read and watched Julia Child, Jacques Pepin, Mario Batali (before the banishment) and a bunch of others. He'd also read just about every book published about the restaurant business.

He first learned chopping and prep from Joey Giamanti. Joey was from Queens, and as an Italian from one of NYC's boroughs, he came from the cradle born to cook -- or at least talk about it as though he was an expert. Joey had chutzpah, nerve, zeal, guts. He saw things others didn't and had the raw nerve to carry through.

When Parker met him in 1975, Joey's big idea was a Chinese-Mexican restaurant in the suburbs of Baltimore. It was a time when there were a few Chinese carry outs and no Mexican restaurants in Baltimore County. A Mexican meal was a box with hard taco shells, yellow plastic cheese, and powdered spices for mixing with ground beef. Two of the greatest culinary inventions ever, flour tortillas and soft corn tortillas, were still a few years away in that part of the country.

At 16, Parker had a heightened curiosity about food, especially ethnic cuisine: Jewish delis, everything Italian, Greek, Chinese, pre-sushi Japanese...almost anything out of the ordinary. So naturally when Joey opened Peking Pancho, he was one of the first to try it out.

As Parker walked toward the counter, Joey stuck his head out from behind the prep station and shouted "Hey kid, wanna job"?

"Umm, maybe. I was just thinking about lunch for now."

"Well, it's not too soon to think about your future."

"I guess so, but why me"?

"You're the first healthy-looking kid to come in here. You got some raggedy-looking youths in this community. You got a job already"?

"Yeah, at Thom McCann's; you know, the shoe store"?

"Oh, Jesus, dealing with those smelly dogs and trying to sell shoe strings and shoe horns to make a quarter extra"?

Shit, he nailed it, thought Parker. "It's not so bad...what's your offer"?

"Two bucks an hour, a free meal for every day you work more than three hours, and skills that will last a lifetime. People will always need food and the vast majority are too lazy to make it themselves. If you're of the philanthropic ilk, you can consider it a public service gig."

Parker looked down at his sneakers, shuffled back and forth along the linoleum floor for a couple of seconds and squeaked "OK, when do I start"?

Ill at the block party

"I told that John Agarn time and time again I didn't want his dog tramplin' and messin' in my yard. After all those warnings, he let the dog out without a leash and he came into my yard -- again! This time I got out my .22 and shot near that dang pooch. I wasn't tryin' to hurt him, just scare him. Well, Agarn must have heard about what happened and he was ill at me. I told him that I'd given fair warnin'."

Hobart Maxwell is telling the story to everyone at the block party after someone innocently mentioned that a new couple had moved into the house formerly owned by Agarn, the lax dog owner.

It's their third block party and they are sensing that it will be the last. Shelly has been relegated to playing with the kids and Parker to smiling and nodding, a clear sign that he's bored out of his wits.

Parker and Shelly shouldn't be at the party to begin with. It's for the block in back of them, but they have friends in one of the houses on that block and their yards were connected until Parker and Shelly put up a fence. They got a lot of compliments on the fence, especially since the best side -- the one without the cross beams -- faced in the direction of the houses behind them. It's a neighborly way to do it according to Shelly.

By the second party, Parker was already tired of explaining why they were there when they didn't live on the block, and the responses, a curt nod of the head, a barely audible hmmm or blink of the eyes were making him feel a bit like the guy wearing a Ravens cap at a Steelers' tailgate party.

On the rare occasion when someone asked Parker what he did, eyes glazed over 20 seconds into his explanation, which he knew was a good and concise one, as he'd tried it out on Shelly before they left for the party. Shelly kept her description as succinct as possible: "I work in IT." She suggested that I just say, "I'm a writer". That was only part of Parker's job but he guessed it covered enough, so they could move on to more important matters. Like "Did you see the State game last night"?

Will Parker: Anti-hero

The hero worship gene must have passed Parker by. He was reading news coverage of grown men and women fawning over a couple of politicians who'd ran for president and failed miserably. What were they getting from this proximity to a couple of guys who were marginally famous? What did it say about them?

When Parker was growing up, he loved some athletes. He went out of his way to get autographs and thought about what it would be like to be them. But he never worshipped them or thought they were better than his parents or even his friends. They just were able to do something he admired very well. But it didn't extend outside of that baseball diamond or that 40x100-foot expanse of hardwood. By the time he was 17, he didn't want to get autographs or even shake hands. A nod or a simple "thanks for what you did" sufficed.

Parker didn't respond to so-called leaders, even as a young boy. So many times he'd heard the Vince Lombardi quote: "Winning isn't everything, it's the only thing." He didn't believe that for a second and couldn't imagine anyone else truly believing it. And if they did, even at age 12 Parker didn't want to be around them.

Was Giuliani a hero after 9/11? What did he do that any other competent mayor wouldn't have done? What's it mean to give a heart-felt speech or provide aid for families from a discretionary budget? Yes, it's good if you can touch hearts and provide relief, but is it heroic?

The myth of the singular leader or innovator in business never gained an inch of traction with Parker, even though he was an entrepreneur, which meant he read countless self-congratulatory articles about how special entrepreneurs are -- how they think differently, work harder, get out of the bed in the morning raring to make a difference, or at the very least move some money around in a way that is extremely profitable. He never felt a bit of that spirit. Parker simply wanted to do what he wanted to do, without sitting in interminable meetings or submitting to people who knew much less about what he was doing and how he was doing it. He was essentially selfish, as he believed most entrepreneurs were.

The only sense of pride and accomplishment he felt was after doing good work and even then, most of his best work wasn't recognized. The praise that mattered was when a peer or a client told him exactly what he did, what it meant to them, and why it was valuable personally or to an organization.

Parker wasn't saving the world. In the best case he was making things a little better for his clients, himself and Shelly. And, unlike Jack Welch or Steve Jobs, he didn't have to screw over or make life miserable for a shipload of others to do it. That was as good as it gets and sat fine with Parker.

Within the nation of pussies

"We've become a nation of pussies!"

Shelly's Uncle Jimmy is reading Carolyn Hax's advice column in *The Washington Post.*

Shelly, standing at the sink with a towel draped over her shoulder, rolls her eyes. She loves her uncle but five days and nights is about two days and nights too long.

"What makes you say that Uncle Jimmy," she monotones, her exasperation clear to Parker, but lost on Jimmy.

"This summabitch can't even summons up the gumption to tell his mother-in-law to quit meddling in his and his wife's parenting. I swear I'd have the screen door hitting her in the ass faster than a Nolan Ryan heater."

"So on that evidence, you're branding the entire nation as pussies?" Shelly is speaking in such a low tone she could be channeling Barry White. This, as Parker knows, signals trouble.

In contrast, Uncle Jimmy's voice is rising to a pitch better suited to Katy Perry.

"Give me a little more credit, darling. Not just this. We got men who can't change a car tire, repair a piece of dry wall, replace a roof shingle, or cook a decent soft-boiled egg." One of these is a square peg, thinks Parker.

"Last week William said he couldn't eat peanuts anymore." William is Uncle Jimmy's youngest son, 31, a very responsible bank manager. "Fucker used to scarf those things down like he was Dumbo. Now he can't eat them? Breaks out in hives? Bunch of shit if you ask me. Last month he paid an extra three bucks for windshield wipers because Autozone does installation for free. Free my ass."

Uncle Jimmy rustles the paper as if he's shaking out a picnic blanket, roughly folds it, bangs it down on the empty dining chair and stalks off to the bathroom for what he calls his "morning constitution".

Shelly snaps the towel she was using to dry the dishes and turns to Parker.

"Well I know one thing. We're having soft-boiled eggs and toast tomorrow morning and Uncle Jimmy's going to be the non-pussified short-order cook."

Corporate strackification

"You know what they say," says Allen Strack casually. "Writers write while others do."

Parker took a deep, inaudible breath. Parker's principal work for Bonsario was writing. Positioning products and the brand so people could understand what they did and why it is important. Telling user success stories in terms with which peers and colleagues could relate. Making the stories aspirational, but without the BS that turns engineers off. Developing clear descriptions of processes and results. Basically, making the products *live*. Pretty simple, really, and Parker had come to think, fairly valuable.

On the other hand, Parker couldn't figure out what Strack, Bonsario's new VP of marketing, did. He talked a lot about framework, focus, workflows, added-value, customer-facing entities, on-time arrival. He had a lot of flow charts, graphs and complex if/when formulations that made Parker feel like a moron and Strack a savant, which was likely the whole point.

Strack had come from a large corporation into a 100-person company with a can-do culture. Bonsario was like the slightly bratty, relentlessly precocious pre-teen that others loved but whom the parents felt had to be controlled in order to become a functioning adult.

The thing was, the company culture worked. Bonsario was turning out products its users loved, more unequivocally than Parker had ever seen. When writing success stories, he didn't have to lead customers into saying great things. They spurted them out like professional wrestlers touting themselves in a post-match interview. Parker had to tone down their quotes or the stories would look like abject puffery.

The normal account executive that disappeared after the sale and came back a month before license renewal was anathema to Bonsario. Its AEs were seemingly always there, not only to set customers on the right track, but to treat them to an after-hours meal, game or show. Support actually meant that.

Bonsario's founders and original Board members looked approvingly at their children and thought they'd make fine adults. But, the outside investors who came in and took over majority share of the company knew better. A company has a proscribed way of maturing and Bonsario needed to get on that path quickly before this "seat-of-the-pants" culture took full hold.

Managers who'd worked their way up through the ranks were sacked for more experienced "professionals" outside the company. A half-dozen Stracks began spaying and neutering the company's operations. Systems were installed. Budgets made iron-clad. Every action needed justification. Approvals that used to take hours took weeks.

Parker leveled his eyes at Strack and after three silent seconds, said evenly: "You know what I do for the company, right? That writing is the central service I offer"?

"Right, so now we're even."

"Even for what"?

"You undermined me last week with Aadhya. You agreed with me when I first proposed the idea of looking into the consumer market, then reversed course when she said it wasn't a good idea."

"I was taking in new information that made me think more critically about the issue. You've never changed your mind based on an additional opinion"?

"Seemed more like a suck-up to the COO and the inability to hold a position."

"I disagree with Aadhya all the time. In fact, it's what makes our relationship work: The ability to disagree without visible resentment and with the same goal in mind."

"Sure, if you say so. Now what can you do to pump up this press release"?

Advice for advice-takers

For good or bad, Parker was a decent listener. The kind of person who helps others advance their stories. The kind who provides small words of succor; unintimidating suggestions prefaced with "One thing you might consider if it makes sense to you..." or "Well, there's one approach that worked for a friend of mine..."

Whether it's a friend or stranger at a bar, Parker tried not to become emotionally involved, but inevitably did and usually dragged Shelly into the conversational aftermath, where her perception of the situation typically aligned with his own. They both liked helping people and were evidently pretty good at it.

Parker knew you shouldn't expect praise, recognition or thanks for helping someone. That's not part of the listening gig. And for the most part he was good with that. But what he realized was that people took his advice like a lozenge, gaining relief and moving on quickly, without feeling the need to circle back and let him know the outcome. Sure, the stranger in the bar isn't going to do that, even if he remembers Parker's advice the next day. But, it would be nice if Andy his former French teacher would close the loop (Did he ever ask out that waitress from the Raw Deals Deli?) or his nephew whose resume he revamped would tell him about the interview, or the sales rep of an ex-client to whom he counseled on how to write and promote a blog would let him know if anything he said helped once he put thoughts to keyboard.

Parker doesn't think he's especially needy, but he does like to find out how the story ends.

The man bun conundrum

"So what's the story with Stevenson"?

Parker is talking to his younger brother, Jack, who coaches college basketball at a Division II school in Ohio. Parker follows Jack's games on web broadcasts and once or twice a year visits him to take in a couple of games in person. Stevenson is a freshman and Jack's second-leading scorer. A good-looking kid if you don't mind the tats, which Parker doesn't. He came from a tough neighborhood in Cleveland, but his mother, a school administrator, kept him on a short leash and monitored his studies with the dedication, zeal and vocal volume of a Marine drill sergeant. Jack had benched Stevenson midway through the first half of last night's game, even though he wasn't in foul trouble. He didn't return to the court until five minutes had elapsed in the second half.

"Whattaya mean"? Jack enjoyed being coy with his older brother.

"Give me a break. You bench your best all-around player and keep him there while the Falcons whittle the lead to three? Kid looked like you punched his dog."

"There were some personal issues."

"Like what, bad hygiene"?

"Let's just say he had some cultural adjustments to make."

"Meaning"?

"He wasn't guarding his man aggressively so I sat him. I got a chance to talk to him one-on-one before we came back out after half-time." Long pause, the kind Jack prefers.

"Anyone ever tell you you're an informational cheapskate"?

"Only you. But you gotta keep this under your hat. He said he couldn't take the guy he was guarding seriously because of the man bun."

"Jesus, that's a first."

"Yeah, for me too and I've been doing this for 20 years."

"Bound to happen sometime I guess. So what did you say to him? Whatever you said worked: He was like a demon once he got back in."

"I told him he doesn't have a choice. He better get over it or forever be known as the Brother who got his ass lit up by a guy with a man bun -- not that there's anything wrong with a man bun."

"Certainly not."

"So how's Shelly"?

Eluding fame two times over

Parker had two shots at fame and fortune earlier in his life. The first was with a tech start-up that would later be sold for half a billion, enriching the first 20 or so employees. He would have been employee number 5. But, he didn't fit in with the three roles that seemed to be required by the company.

One role was Parker as a creative genius with an original vision so strong it couldn't be denied. He'd met a few of the rare individuals who could do that, and knew he wasn't one of them. He was very good at refining a vision, communicating it, making it something to which people could relate, but not at initiating the magic idea.

The second role was as the unflagging disciple, ready, willing and able to not only swallow, but inculcate and cheerlead for, the company kool-aid. As an atheist, a not-all-in team member (he could never stand behind a teammate if he did something that was flat-out wrong), and not a complete believer in any political movement, going along with the program for better or worse wasn't in his DNA.

The third role didn't fit either: The rebel who is so bright, so insouciant, that he wins over the admiration (and latent resentment that can't be acted upon) of every one above him in the company; the guy who surfs whenever it is damn well best to surf, no matter the corporate demands. The guy who'll walk if given any shit and will likely land at a competitor. The one destined to make a fortune; it's just a matter of where and when. Parker, a lapsed Catholic but a Catholic nonetheless, had too much guilt for that one.

The other shot was music. He'd developed a voice, a way with lyrics, and a facile approach with a rhythm guitar. So much so that a local lead singer wanted him to be second voice and rhythm guitarist for her band -- a very good band that made its members a decent living and is still a thriving institution.

Parker turned that one down on the grounds that he would invariably fall in love with the lead singer and it would turn out badly. It was a conceited notion, he knew -- she had a long-time boyfriend and no apparent romantic interest in him and Parker had been with Shelly for about six months and didn't want to blow it.

But, he remembered falling in love with woman singers from a distance, including one in Nashville who was his cousin's friend. He met her before the show and when she started singing during the show he felt as if he was floating in some delicious syrup, his mind anesthetized with quiet joy.

He grinned unnervingly like a lunatic. Leaning over to his cousin Jack he whispered, "I'm glad I didn't know she sang like this when you introduced me or I would have offered to buy her a condo, whether she needed one or not."

Uncle Jimmy's big tater

"Where you going"?

"Out for a smoke."

"But it's tied and there's only three minutes left."

"Well, you know what they say, basketball is just the last two minutes."

"Screw you," Parker muttered. Shelly's Uncle Jimmy pushing his buttons again. They'd had the argument before, Parker calling out Jimmy, saying all sports come down to the last inning or couple of minutes, but there are patterns established before that; patterns that help dictate the outcome. Has the point guard established he can beat his man off the dribble or has a defensive player spotted a weakness, like the ball handler exposing the ball for a split second when he goes left, or the big man in the post feels his man overplaying on his right hip, leaving an opening for him to spin to the left and get to the baseline for a layup? Little things during the course of a game can lead to big things at the end.

Parker's articulate case for the efficacy of watching a total game of basketball always elicited the same response from Uncle Jimmy.

"Last two minutes," he'd say with a half-smile and wry shake of the head.

Not that Uncle Jimmy was without insights. One time he and Parker were watching the O's Chris Davis strike out for the third time in a game.

"It's a little like inventing," said Jimmy.

"Baseball or Chris Davis striking out"? asked Parker.

"Both, but Davis epitomizes what the inventor goes through. Failure after failure, hundreds sometimes, until you get the big hit, the grand salami."

"Didn't know you had studied the inventing game, Uncle Jimmy."

"Didn't just study, I practiced it. Still do."

"And did you ever get that big tater, that grand salami"?

"Yep. Nothing Edison-like, but Ron Propeil would have proudly pitched it."

"So, educate me, grand guru."

"That immersion blender you used to scramble the eggs this morning? I invented the basic mechanics and patented their ass. Sold it to Waring for a decent ROI."

"Wow. You're immortal. Always wondered how you got that place at the beach."

"And a whole lot of other shit nobody knows about."

"Damn, you a bad mutha..."

"Shut your mouth."

To disagree is human

Parker always tries to be likeable, helpful; a guy who will go the extra mile to please someone. But, he always found someone in the business world whom he annoyed. More than a couple of times, these people were in a position to do something about it.

Most of the time it had to do with power. Specifically, a disagreement with someone who wanted power. The disagreement wasn't a big deal to Parker. In most cases, he didn't even know the problem existed until it came to a head. Disagreement was a fact of life in Parker's mind. He had come from a family of disagreers. Without it, there would have been little basis for conversation in his family.

What he'd discovered, was that for certain people in business, and he suspected in their personal lives as well, even what appeared to Parker to be benign disagreement was considered mutinous. Certain people carried disagreements around like chips in a casino, marshalling them, building a pile, until finally ready to dispose of them in a series of seemingly reckless actions.

These people assumed that Parker wanted power in the same way they did. But he didn't. He just wanted his opinion heard and considered. And, of course he thought he was right almost all the time -- who didn't?

It finally occurred to Parker that people in business are no different from kids on the playground growing up -- the ones who own a ball and if they can't get their way, take the ball and head home. Parker's reaction hasn't changed since he was a kid: "Screw them. I'll find another ball and keep playing."

The power of like

Shelly didn't know about love. Even as a kid she'd rejected bromides like the Beatles "All You Need is Love". Yes, that and enough money to subsidize the next four generations of your family and friends.

She thinks she loves Parker, but isn't absolutely certain. Whoever knows? She thinks sometimes the concept of love has to be inculcated in you from the time you are born, like the Bible or a political doctrine. Even then, is that smile that comes to your face automatically when he walks into the room love or just some other kind of animal attraction? Is that gush of warmth that infuses her body when she's in his arms love, lust or simple comfort, no different from the feeling of sitting in front of a fire when the world outside is covered in frost?

She tells Parker she loves him all the time. Why not? It makes them both feel good, and as far as she knows it's true.

What Shelly does know for certain is the power of *like*. She likes almost everything about Parker. Had from the beginning, before even seeing him. His voice on the phone was interested, engaged, warm, smart but not haughty. Yes, he could be a self-absorbed prick at times, but that seemed more a matter of becoming immersed in work or play; or highly animated about a line of thought. And it's temporary -- he can be pulled back into the greater world with a few well-chosen words: Not so much what she says but how she says it. She's mapped his terrain and it's overall very hospitable.

Shelly thinks like is a much more powerful binding element than love. She knows many couples who loved one another but couldn't sustain a relationship because despite the mutual attraction, one or the other had something fundamental they didn't like about the other or they didn't agree with in a major way. That stuff always comes out. Maybe not right away, but as hobbies and interests diverge, or the kids get older, or outside influences tug at the couple's tenuous threads.

Right alongside like is trust in Shelly's mind. Parker is an attractive man and she's no limburger herself. But there's never been doubt from either. The trust extends to other things people don't talk about, but that can pull at those threads: Chiefly, money; how it's spent, distributed, saved or not saved. Shelly and Parker, without belaboring it, are always on the same financial page; both were brought up to not spend beyond their needs, but also to treat themselves well if the money is available.

The other thing about like and trust: they're solid. When the flame dampens down to an ember, she and Parker will still be laughing, liking and trusting.

Knowing when to fold 'em

Peking Poncho faces east and on this mid-morning in spring shafts of light, redolent with dancing dust particles, streamed through the glass door and front windows.

Will Parker, 16, walked to work that morning. It was a day made for friendliness, the air crisp as a newly picked green apple. Everything sparked with energy. Parker walked with a bounce, waving to barber Bill as he walked by his shop, which always smelled of alcohol, both from Bill's breath and the solution in which he dipped his combs. Through all the signs advertising the Roffler method, Bill gave Parker a rare nod, and a minute tip of his feathering scissors.

Even within the cars streaming by on Hanson Street, a two-lane highway with no sidewalk, on which every car routinely exceeded the speed limit by 10 or 15 miles per hour and were never pulled over, drivers seemed more benign, bopping their heads to tunes on the radio. Parker caught bits of "Love Her Madly" by the Doors and "Theme from Shaft", which added a switch in his hips to the bounce in his step. Even the wisp of a Marlboro from a passing car smelled fresh and inviting.

He was prepping for the lunch run, tipping snow peas and snipping spring onions for the Moo Goo Gai Burrito and the Lo Mein Mexicana when Joey Giamanti burst in the door, letting in a stream of cool air. He was big man and he strode into a room like an oversized Cagney, displacing whatever and whoever was there.

"Well, the gig's up, my man," he shouted in mid-stride. "After lunch, this joint's history."

Parker stopped his knife in mid-rocking motion, which he'd learned from Joey, who'd learned it as a teenager from precocious and illegal visits to a basement prep area of a four-star French place irreverently placed in Flushing before the owners came to their Gallic senses.

"What"? It was all Parker could muster.

"Sorry man, but I'm closin' up this place. It's a great concept and a righteous program, but this part of the world (sweeping his arms in a wide arc) just ain't ready for the likes of me."

"But, where are you going? What will you do? What's going to happen to Toni?" Parker almost blushed when he asked about Toni, Joey's girlfriend. She'd come down with him from Queens and visited the restaurant sometimes near closing time, teetering in on stacked heels, an off-the-shoulder blouse with a push-up bra that exposed cleavage that would challenge the Pope not to stare.

"She's comin' with. We're going back to the borough. Remember when I went back up there two weeks ago, when I saw the boys in pinstripes ground your fine feathered friends? Well, I saw something there that got my juices flowing."

"What, Horace Clarke and Jake Gibbs"?

"Actually I'm a little sweet on that boy Palmer you have on the mound, but you've made me digress, you little asshole. There's something going down in the borough that won't be denied. This thing we did here, it's OK, but it'll likely limp along for another year before taking off into franchise-land or dying, and I don't have the time; places to go, people to see, mountains to climb, money to make, etc., etc."

Parker realized his hand was shaking so he set aside the 10-inch knife.

"So what's this next big thing"?

"I'm on the number 7 and take the 52nd Street stop. I had to see a man about a horse. It was rush hour and people are coming home from work. All kinds of people -- your Orientals, umm Asians, whites, blacks, Ricans, you name it. Two blocks from the stop there's this hole in a wall joint, about the size of a few phone booths stuck together. They got a window opening to the street and a line of people waiting outside -- every age, socio-economic group, size, shape, ethnicity -- waiting for food. It's like the beer stand at Yankee Stadium. I'm thinking 'what's the deal'? And get this, the sign on the top of the window says "Indo-Chinese Cuisine". I ask a little cutie in the line, 'what's the Indo stand for'? She says, 'Indian. It's a mix of Indian and Chinese food -- hot, spicy and good.' I ask her what she's gettin' and she says 'Chicken 65', so I get in line and order some. Turns out to be chunks of chicken rolled into a spice mix and deep fat fried with peppers and onions. Shit rocks like a fuckin' hurricane; endorphins sparkin' like a motherfucker. I'm thinking, 'this is it, the shit'. So I wait around, talk to the owner, whose mother is the cook. They're Indians, you know, from India. Delhi, specifically. This guy, Raj, tells me that this is the new thing. Chinese love it, Indians love it, and he says, modest as can be, 'Americans appear to love it'. So, I ask him, 'How would you like to get out of this bandbox and start a real restaurant'. He says he doesn't know what this bandbox thing is, but yes, he'd like a restaurant, with real dishes, silverware, laminated chopsticks for those so inclined. I say 'done' and the next day I'm signing on the dotted line for a former Czech joint that lost its lease. The rest, as they say, will be history."

"Damn, man, that's great, I think...but what'll I do"?

"Ah, shit man, you'll be fine. I'm payin' you for two more weeks as you help me move. You have skills, son, that'll get you a job in almost any restaurant around. You have a *trade* and ain't half bad for a Ballmer boy. Most of all, you're a young, healthy, white male who'll get a college education. You're the one-percent of the luckiest people alive."

"Actually I'm Catholic."

"Me too, my man, but that makes no difference anymore. A Catholic was elected president years ago and he and his brother died for our sins. You have no excuses for not being a master of the universe."

Dog-gone Parker

Parker likes dogs, but not indiscriminately, which based on cursory evidence puts him at odds with the vast majority of suburban white people in America. He's thinking this while walking through something called the Midtown Festival in the small downtown of Cary, NC. (Midtown is about 100 yards from downtown by Parker's estimate.)

Festivals are now everywhere, this one marking the first anniversary of a local brewery. And where there are festivals, there are dogs. All kinds of pooches -- tall, short, straight- and curly-haired, stubby, elongated, with pushed in snouts and sleek long ones like the hood of an old Hudson. They have one thing in common: Their owners are exceedingly proud. While the dogs aren't wearing sashes like beauty contestants, they are adorned with an array of scarfs, t-shirts and even hip hats. The owners are like Colonel Parkers, doing everything but giving out 8x10 glossies with paw prints.

When he walks around his neighborhood, which he does at least three times a week, Parker encounters a lot of dogs. There's the one who hides until he walks by his yard, then sprints out barking like a demented seal. He always screeches to a halt at the edge of the property, probably courtesy of an invisible electronic fence. Parker's gotten used to this one -- muttering "rat bastard" under his breath helps.

When Parker walks, he wants to walk. It's exercise. He doesn't listen to music, make phone calls or text. It's both physical and mental therapy. Occasionally he'll stop and talk with a neighbor, although he's secretly annoyed by the intrusion into his inner dialog.

What he never wants to do is stop and pet a dog with which he has no relationship. But owners seem to expect him to do this, thrusting the dog into Parker's personal space and making him feel guilty if he doesn't pet the dog or mew over it.

Parker thinks it makes a lot of sense not to pet and fawn over someone else's dog. First off, it's not his dog; you don't know where it's been or how it behaves. You don't know if Danny Boy will pick up on some kind of scent and just haul off and bite your ass. But most of all, Parker sees it as a personal intrusion. What if, Parker thinks, he just reached down and starting patting the head and mussing the hair of every strange kid that crossed his path? Or gave a hug to every woman walking with her boyfriend or husband? Or gave another man a pat on the ass as you would a teammate? Would that be acceptable societal behavior?

Parker relayed all this to Shelly one night over a bottle of red. She listened patiently and replied, "Do you think you might be overthinking this a bit"?

If the genes fit, wear them

Shelly's sister Jenny was getting on her last nerve. It happened as always, after a couple glasses of wine around the kitchen table, after Parker and Jenny's husband Rick repaired to the den for scotch and an NBA game. Shelly thought about asking Parker to not let her be alone with her sister, but she didn't visit that often, and she is her sister after all.

It starts with childhood stories. Their mom scolding Fred, the family's black Lab, after he chewed up her collection of Life magazines with Elvis on the cover. Or the time their father hid their brother Joe's baseball mitt after he left it outside one summer night. And Shelly's prom date, who got so drunk and/or stoned in the afternoon before the big event that he tumbled down the stairs while their dad was taking pictures, severely spraining his ankle and throwing up on the front-door entry rug.

Then, with the inevitability of the tides or sunset, Jenny launches into it.

"You know what I never understood"? (Yes, I know all too well, thinks Shelly). "Why our whole family, not just mom and dad, but our aunts, uncles and cousins, thought you were the artistic one -- that you had the sole creativity genes in the family."

"I never thought that."

"No, but you went along with it. I mean, yeah, you played clarinet and guitar, painted lovely landscapes, wrote poems and short stories, but I did creative stuff too. What the hell was up with that"?

Shelly turns to the sink and busies herself with dishes. They could have waited, but she needs the distraction. And she can't look Jenny in the face when she goes on this screed. Jenny was an honor student through high-school and college. She's an attorney with two girls who graduated summa cum laude from Harvard. Both

39

are already pulling down big green, one at a law firm, the other at a tech start-up. By all accounts, Rick is a caring and responsible husband.

"We couldn't have a family get-together without 'Play a song for us, Shelly' or 'read that new poem your mom was telling us about'. It was like I imagine it is being Gisele Bündchen's twin sister who's not nearly as hot or Clint Howard, you know Ron's younger brother who doesn't direct films and always plays the creepy guy"?

Shelly swings around, red-faced, and whispers softly, teeth clenched and diction clipped: "I'm sorry your life hasn't been absolutely perfect, Jenny, and you can't help but focus on the one tiny element of your upbringing for which you don't think you received proper credit. You were -- are -- a good writer and singer and probably should have received more recognition for creativity. But as a younger sister you eclipsed me in everything -- as a student, as a career professional, as a parent, and one day as a grandparent. So why can't you leave one small crumb of glory on the plate for me"?

Jenny lets out an exaggerated giggle, throws her arms in the air and in mock-Streisand voice croons: "It had to be you, it had to be you..."

The people's people person

Everybody loves Shelly, and for good reason. She engages nearly everyone: waitstaff, checkout people, plumbers, electricians. If competent and not racist or sexist, anyone who comes to the house to work becomes an acquaintance. By the end of an hour, Shelly knows where they live, their family, hobbies and the peccadilloes of their jobs.

All the people who are faceless to others are living, breathing, sentient beings who Shelly, in her unquenchable but caring curiosity, wants to engage.

Sometimes the conversation with everybody annoys Parker. Like when he wants to get in and out of the grocery store. Or he wants to order his own wine without input from the waiter who is barely drinking age and likely spends more time hunched over a PBR than a chalky Chablis. But, when he gets upset, he knows he's being a cad. He also realizes that he gets this level of personal caring every day, almost every hour, and how much he misses it when he's separated from Shelly.

Parker has heard many individuals characterized as a "people person," and most of the times he doesn't necessarily agree with that assessment. Or maybe he just has a different definition of the term. Most of the so-called people persons he'd met were simply loquacious; they start conversations as a means to talk about themselves or as a preamble to a one-way discourse on a favorite subject, whether it be their boat, their kids, their favorite team, or their pet political views. They are people with a plan that centers on themselves.

Shelly is a best-of-breed people person. She wants to know about the person. Period. If she has any ulterior motive at all it is to get the person out of their sometimes boring, sometimes ritualistic routine -- to make them feel like interesting people who have a life. She does it easily, naturally, and the response is almost always a smile. Not many people are built that way, and Parker feels exceedingly lucky that he is loved by one who is.

Parker's superlative dilemma

"He's the best."

"The greatest of all time. The GOAT."

"Genius. Certified fucking genius."

"He rates among the top 5 at worst."

"Her taste is unequalled."

"That's the best restaurant in the city."

At one time or another, Parker has heard all these superlatives. And they all made him uncomfortable. But people, especially men, somehow need to rank, quantify, place on a rung practically any form of human endeavor.

It's uniquely American, thinks Parker, to make everything a competition; even things that seem intrinsically uncompetitive: art, music, food preparation, survival.

In North Carolina, rating native food specialties is an active pastime. The best barbecue (both eastern and western). The best shrimp and grits. The best mac and cheese. Parker loves all those things, but how do you judge one of them the best? Maybe it's a lack of imagination on his part, but just how good can pimento cheese be beyond really, really good?

Then there is the singular inventor. In a world where invention is always in the air and people are constantly building on others' creations, exchanging ideas, talking even when they are supposed to be keeping secrets, how can there be a single inventor of anything?

Parker does believe in a sort of karmic convergence or some kind of brewing ideas that circulate in the air waiting to be plucked and developed into something new and different. But that's something different. That's innovation or simply evolution or maybe just plain old vanilla development. Almost everything, especially today, is the product of group-think, whether acknowledged or not.

Parker used to go on with his mother about ratings of esoteric things. She could boil things to an essence that Parker couldn't. Her take: "If it makes people happy, why do you care? The only rankings that matter to me right now are how many games the O's are ahead of the Yankees and whether the TV ratings are good enough to keep Tom Jones on the air."

Jimmy's recipe for dissatisfaction

"Could you leave that alone for just 15 minutes so we can enjoy the greatest time of day the Good Lord ever invented."

Parker looks up from his phone. He is on the back patio with Uncle Jimmy sipping scotch at what is indeed the most beautiful time of day, when sunlight is giving up its last light and yielding to night. If there was any doubt that birds are social creatures, it's dispelled at this time of day, when they are chirping and singing passionately, seemingly setting up their assignations for the evening.

"Spend enough time on-line and you'll be dissatisfied about everything," says Jimmy. "Your mate's bust line, her willingness to have sex, your physique, your financial position, your social life, and most pointedly, your dick size."

"Dick size"?

"I'm not a luddite. After Julie died, I spent a lot of time online, seeking something or other, and it ended up mostly with porn. Every man was hung like Marky Mark in that what's-you-call-it movie."

"Boogie Nights"?

"Yeah, that's the one. You're just begging to feel inadequate."

"Well, I mostly just keep track of friends on Facebook."

"Well, that has its own brand of shaming. There's a reason it's called Facebook -- everybody is putting on their own best face. You're almost always going to feel their lives are better than yours -- they go out more often, travel better, eat at nicer restaurants, and spend their free time doing culturally edifying shit, while you're picking up pine cones in your backyard. It's a recipe for dissatisfaction. Like the man said, 'I'd rather pound my own dick with a hammer.'"

"Who's that man"?

"Direct quote from an artist friend of mine when I asked him why he doesn't go after local government commissions."

A lying laggard

Parker never lies. Not necessarily because of exceptionally high moral standards or his Catholic upbringing. He definitely thinks honesty is good, but when it comes down to it, he probably doesn't lie for a simple reason: He's no good at it.

It isn't as if he had never tried. He tried when he was younger and failed miserably. He had several sterling lying-ass role models, but could never make it sound natural or overcome the guilt. His delivery was a dead give-away: eyes averted, hands rubbing together, voice rising, exaggerated umbrage.

His lack of lying acumen reminds Parker of the old prison joke.

It's lights out in a prison cellblock and a new guy is settling down to sleep. It's quiet for a while until a guy yells out "11" and everybody breaks into laughter. Another guy calls out "2" and there are more peals of laughter.

The new guy turns to his cellmate and asks what that's about. The cellmate explains, "Everybody here knows the jokes so well that we just call out a number."

The new guy says "I'm gonna give that a try." He calls out "9".

Crickets.

"What happened," asks the new guy.

"Well, some guys can tell a joke and some guys can't," answers the cellmate.

Come to think of it, Parker can't tell a decent joke either.

Sunny and miserable

Parker and Shelly sat out on the patio wearing hats and light jackets in the waning sunlight. It's 55 degrees and there's still snow in the shadows from the night before, when the Triangle area of North Carolina had gotten about an inch of powder, then ice. As usual, it quickly disappeared, mirage-like, the next day, except for some small pockets in heavily shaded areas.

The snow reminded Parker of a ski trip with a woman named Sunny a few years before he met Shelly. He'd met Sunny in unusual circumstances for him: At a bar where she was a waitress. He'd never been one with a fast line and the type of brimming confidence that would make the kind of score that men mythologize. He had what his friend Manny called "a parlor rap". Pretty good in one-on-one situations where he had some quiet time to unravel stories, but almost useless in the rapid-fire battleground of the bar. But somehow, this night, it worked with Sunny, despite the relentless assault of aged disco and glam-rock in the adjoining club. They'd made out in the parking lot, exchanged phone numbers, and when he called, she responded. Miracle upon miracle.

They'd been seeing each other for about five months when Sunny invited Parker to join her family for a weekend in a large chalet owned by her uncle in Deep Creek Lake, Maryland. It was ski season and Parker had tried skiing on some icy slopes in southern Pennsylvania, so it sounded OK.

Almost from the beginning, it was doomed. It wasn't quite "Guess Who's Coming to Dinner," especially since there were no persons of color involved, but it was close in vibe and awkwardness. The biggest difference was that whereas Katherine Houghton, Sidney Poitier's fiancé in the movie, was lovingly supporting, the inaptly named Sunny treated Parker as an outcast nearly immediately. Parker didn't help matters by, in an effort to curry favor, volunteering to shovel snow in the driveway in sub-zero wind chill and getting his ill-shod feet frostbitten. He had to warm his toes by the fire for 30 minutes with Sunny's tut-tutting grandmother while Sunny, her brother and cousins went off to a neighbor's basement for illegal fun.

The next day was nearly apocalyptic for Parker. He had to start at the beginner's slope, a very unmanly development. When he progressed to the intermediate slope he looked like Buster Keaton rehearsing pratfalls. Meanwhile, Sunny, who had zero athletic ability, blithely coasted on by, not by cutting back and forth, but by doing the plow with V-shaped skis. She occasionally waved at him with a mittened hand like a beauty queen sitting on top of a convertible seat coasting down Main Street at 10 mph in a small-town Christmas parade.

During a break in the humiliation, Parker was hanging in the lounge and saw two couples who were friends of his older cousins. He practically threw pride to the considerable winds of Deep Creek and begged them to let him stay with them and drive him back home the next day. But, he stayed the course for another miserable day and a silent ride back to Sunny's house with a car full of her relatives and Parker's skin still vibrating from hours of exposure to the cold for which he wasn't appropriately dressed.

Parker knew he was sadly, tragically needy when they got back and he continued to try to call Sunny. She was a receptionist at her father's accounting firm and refused to take his calls. He finally resigned himself to losing the only woman he had ever picked up at a bar.

Shelly listened to the story intently, shaking her head in sympathy with Parker's distress, but at the end she sighed and said, "You're generally a wise man, Will, but in some matters it's as if you just fell off the turnip truck."

"What do you mean"?

"You should have known not to date a woman named 'Sunny'."

"And how would I know that"?

"'Joy', 'Sunny', 'Daisy', 'April'...why do you think they have those names? It's because they are the apples of their parents' eyes. They can do little wrong and everything marginally right that they do is going to be magnified by that gauzy lens of parental adoration and propriety. They were born to be spoiled. You should have high-tailed out of that bar the moment you heard her name."

"Damn, another reason why I wish I would have met you sooner."

Parker's bromides for life

"I'm putting together a collection of Parker bromides," says Shelly, stretching out on the bed in the morning light. She and Parker had nowhere urgent to go, so they had the luxury of stretching, yawning, hugging, telling lazy stories under the sheets.

"OK, hit me."

"Things never happen for a reason."

"True enough. Next."

"Leaders never talk about leadership and players never talk about playing."

"Word."

"Always be suspicious of anyone who places a big premium on posture."

"Don't remember that one, but I like it."

"All for one is always bad for at least a few ones."

"I think some of these are yours...let's quit while there's still some headroom."

"Suit yourself, big boy, but I got Escalade-like headroom."

"To be continued then..."

The French dance party

Shelly and her mom, a 70-year-old widow named Nancy who lives about a half-mile away, have become best friends. This is after a childhood where Shelly rebelled against Nancy's strict definitions of what a girl should be, how a teenager should act and dress, and the path a young adult should take career- and relationship-wise.

But eventually, especially after Shelly's Dad died 10 years earlier, they reconciled. They discovered that each could use a little of what the other had: In Nancy's case, her daughter's humor and loosely managed chaos. In Shelly's case, her mother's historical recall and finely tuned observational powers.

Nancy is taking French lessons for an upcoming trip to the "mother country" as she now calls it, although there is scant evidence of her ancestral connections to that region of the world. But, as Shelly points out, it's tons more romantic than Lithuania.

So, every Thursday night after work, Nancy drives over to Shelly and Parker's house to do dialogs. Shelly studied French in high school and spent a month in South of France after college graduation, so she's fairly well versed in the language, but she also wanted a refresher. As a token of appreciation, Nancy comes armed with some fine boxed wine and a cheese platter from Harris Teeter.

At first, the two showed admirable discipline, exchanging dialog for 45 minutes until breaking out the wine. Then it was a half-hour. Then 15 minutes. Then, fuck it, wine is part of everyday socializing in France, why not share hospitality from the get-go?

The French lessons have become the wobbly foundation for a two-person party. A little French, a little cheese, a lot of wine and old stories, 20 minutes of frantic dancing to Motown and Bruno Mars, and raucous laughter throughout.

Parker typically stops at the gym after work on Thursdays. When he arrives home, about 7:30 p.m. or so, Shelly and her mom are sprawled limp-limbed on the floor, their backs against the sofa, wine box on the rug, wine glasses tilting loosely in their hands, LPs strewn around them, and "Murder She Wrote" on TV.

"Hey Parker," they yell like giddy, collusive school girls, "want some wine big boy"?

Parker shakes his head, gets out the menu from the local pizza delivery joint and settles in for a martini, but only one: In about an hour and a half, he'll drive Nancy home in her car and walk the eight blocks back to his house.

Breaching the last bastion

"Well, Jay-sus, that'll set back sex a few more decades," says Shelly's Uncle Jimmy. He and Parker are watching a commercial for one of those adjustable mattresses with separate settings for each side of the bed.

"The bed," says Jimmy, sipping his Elijah Craig whisky with a splash of Blenheim hot ginger ale, "is the last bastion of shared territory for a couple. How can sex or even cuddling happen when each side has to have his and her, his and his, her and her, or trans and him or her unique settings? Once they get indoctrinated into their individualized settings, how much time can they spend together enduring one or the other's setting? After sex, in your case three minutes, it'll immediately be 'Thanks, but I need to get back to my setting'. There's enough perfunctory got-damn sex in the world without more incentive to go back to your respective corners, with your individualized bed setting whispering in your ear."

"Wow, you've thought through this, Jimmy," says Parker, in slight awe.

"Looky here, young blood. A big part of being in a relationship is being uncomfortable sometimes. It's the sacrifice you make to accommodate your partner, hoss. You gotta navigate unfamiliar territory and sometimes that starts in bed: Sleeping on the opposite side of the bed from her, even if you like her side of the bed; dealing with the pillow bruhaha, which has become a big deal; deciding whether you need a blanket or not; jammies or no jammies -- it's all part of the tapestry. It sounds quaint, but intimacy comes, eventually, at its own good-ole time, from initial discomfort. Remove the accommodation and you might as well be two pigs in a pen."

Caving in to the PNO

"Got another one of those ambush calls today," says Shelly. She's sautéing onions, peppers, chilis and garlic for a favorite, low-maintenance meal: Cheese and spinach enchiladas. She and Parker both make this meal, generally in the same way, using canned sauce augmented by freshly chopped tomatoes or Shelly's world-beating marinara when there's some on hand. Four large enchiladas give them each two meals. The leftovers are coveted and sometimes don't make it past breakfast the following morning, especially if fresh eggs are on hand.

"Who this time"? asks Parker. He'd done all the chopping and is now grating some Havarti.

"Usual suspects," Shelly replies. She's an IT person for a trade association website. The "usual suspects" typically mean marketing or sales, whom Shelly calls the PNOs, Perpetually Needy Ones. Parker listens hard when Shelly tells these stories because he could easily be defined as a PNO.

It isn't what the PNOs ask, but the way they ask it and the timing that typically irk Shelly. At least that's Parker's take on it.

"Starts out with the token compliment -- 'I really like the new menu structure or that photo you put up last week, very creative'. They sound so phony I can't believe they believe it themselves, but they're shameless. Some more small talk, like the pole-vaulter warming up. Then he starts sprinting down the path, erect pole in the air: 'I have a big ask.' 'Yes, you do have a big ass', I'm thinking. But I'm silent like Steve McQueen, baby. Always good to upset the equilibrium a bit. He hits the launch pad and starts to rise in the air: 'I need the new sales brochure up this afternoon.'

"This afternoon? You know it's already 4 on Friday, right, and I leave early to beat the weekend beach traffic, right?"

"I said it was a big ask, but can you just say yes to this? The team will really appreciate it. We have a sales meeting tomorrow and it would be a killer to show this to the client."

"So, buttons pushed: compliment, humbling request, team player, client meeting the next day. Which, given it's a Saturday, probably means golf, lunch and drinks. So I wait a few beats, just to give myself some dignity before I cave in. 'Yes', I sigh, 'but you better think good things about me when you're in the clubhouse with that BLT and bloody mary with that stalk of celery and hit of tabasco.'"

"Oh I will, kind woman, I will."

Eric Burdon makes it real

"This kind of show is a disservice to older singers," says Parker.

He and Shelly are watching Jay and the Americans on a 60s revival show airing as part of a PBS fundraiser. They're both suckers for these shows, although they know the voices are going through a distilling and homogenization process that would pass FDA muster, back when the FDA meant something.

"I think he sounds great," says Shelly. "It's amazing."

"But the guy only has to come out and do a couple of songs at full blast, singing through a shit-load of processors, then he gets to have his oxygen, collapse on the sofa and not worry about it for another year or so. I feel bad for the guys in their 60s and 70s who do this kind of thing night after night and have people say 'Oh his voice is shot'.

"You're referring to Brian with this right"? Shelly knows Parker is sensitive to any criticism about Brian Wilson, especially around voice deterioration. She loves Brian too, and likes his nearly 80 year-old voice just fine.

"Not just Brian; others too. Men and women both. Their voice can't migrate into a lower octave without people saying they should hang it up. They need to perpetually have the voice of a 20- or 30-year-old. I know the audience is craving nostalgia like a moon pie, but wouldn't it be nice if the singers could evolve the song a bit, instead of doing a rote repetition -- put a little age on it."

"Yeah, I know what you mean. A whole life is in those 60- or 70-year-old voices. Time served, places seen, experiences, life its own damn self. Pretty weird to see these guys like they've been preserved in wax with youthful voice intact."

After the fund-raising break, which now includes young people whose parents weren't even born when those acts were making their hay, the show returns, with Eric Burdon taking the stage. He sings in a hoarse voice about two registers lower than the original "It's My Life". But with gusto and passion -- he's killing it.

"That's what I'm talking about," says Parker.

"Sounds like he's lived "It's My Life" says Shelly.

The ethnic restaurant report

"I don't know about this place; not a lot of Africans here," says Shelly.

She and Parker are freshly seated at a small corner table at an Ethiopian restaurant. Judging by the maracas and serapes on the wall the place hasn't yet made a decor trip across the Atlantic from Mexico.

"So are Africans compelled to go to an Ethiopian restaurant?" asks Parker.

"Well, you know how Janey and others always comment that a Chinese restaurant must be good if there are a lot of Chinese people eating there?" Janey worked with Shelly and trafficked in clichés to a point where Parker thought it was satire, although Shelly assured him it was "for real, man".

"I mean, why isn't that standard applied to other restaurants," says Shelly. "Nobody says a Greek restaurant must be good because there are a lot of Greek people eating there. Same goes for an Italian or German place."

"Well, it might be because Chinese are more readily identifiable," reasons Parker.

"Maybe, but they don't necessarily say that about a soul food joint. And I think equating quality to the number of people from an ethnic group at the restaurant might be a bit specious. It's assuming that all Chinese people go to good Chinese restaurants. Are they all gourmands, knowing who makes the best chicken feet? Are they all like the Italians from Long Island or Jersey who emerge from the womb as pizza experts? Maybe the Chinese hang at a restaurant because it reminds them of the food they grew up with, whether it was great food or not. Remember that so-called comfort food restaurant in Baltimore that was mediocre at best but people still flocked to it because of the pit beef?"

"Yeah, but that was owned by an ex-Baltimore Raven, so it's extenuating circumstances. It's almost a law that any restaurant owned by an athlete or ex-athlete has to be mediocre. Anything different would upset the cosmos."

"But how about if the restaurant owner is just a popular person, maybe with an extended family and a big role in the Chinese community? They could come to the restaurant out of loyalty. Or maybe the owner is a loan shark and part of paying the debt is eating at his so-so restaurant. Or maybe, more charitably, he's one of those hospitable bastards, the kind people like to be around, and if the food is just average, well that's alright?"

"You make a strong case that might bear investigating," says Parker, scooping up some doro wat with a spongy piece of injera. "I say we canvas every ethnic restaurant in a 10-mile radius and then write a report."

"It's a deal," says Shelly, clinking her wine glass to Parker's beer bottle. "But can we dispense with the report?"

When Parker misses smoking

"Well, the highland whiskies are more mellow, gentle on the palate, almost feminine. I like them, so you could call me a feminist, heh heh. You can have all that peatiness; I mean that stuff is the basis for coal, right? So if you want to ingest coal, be my guest. As for me, I enjoy a *refined* tipple."

Steven Hester delivers the last line in what he thinks is a British accent. He punctuates it by raising his pinkie as he lifts the amber liquid to his mouth.

Hester thinks his golfing and attorney-ing skills spill over into other topics: music, politics, culture, art -- anything really. In his mind, his is a unique take, superior to all others sitting around a table, at a bar, in a meeting, or within a foursome. He has his acolytes, of course, that fawn over him to reinforce that notion: junior lawyers, his wife and her lesser posse, caddies and others who think golf skills make the man.

Hester has a veneer of knowledge about nearly everything, and the voice and confidence to suggest that he is just skimming the surface. But Parker knows that the surface is it, like what looks like an NYC brownstone neighborhood at Universal Studios in Florida, until you see it's a prop, a big boarded backstop.

"So I grab this guitar from the stand during the band's break and start playing 'Wagon Wheel' right? Well, the guitarist is starting to have a fit, but then he listens and nods along. Evidently, I'm nailing it! And who do you think walks into the bar just as I'm starting the second chorus"?

"Dylan"? Parker nearly snarls, although it's lost on Hester.

"Close enough, my man, close enough, but no cigar. It's Ketch friggin' Secor, who co-wrote the song with Dylan and made it into a hit with Old Crow Medicine Show! He walks right up, puts his head against mine and chimes in on the chorus. Turned the bar out, I'm telling you!"

Parker leans into Shelly and whispers, "It's times like these I wish I still smoked."

The curse of muscular memory

Good memory is seen as a sign of heightened intellect. Older people are encouraged to read to stimulate it. Youngsters are encouraged to memorize as an intellectual strength-building exercise.

Nobody talks about when the memory muscle becomes too strong; when it decides to hijack present thoughts; when it hands over prime real estate to the awful memories, those you're perpetually trying to stuff back into the suitcase. Parker would sometimes give his right nut for a lesser functioning memory.

Brand, baby, brand

"You need to start promoting yourself, man."

This from Steve Jankowski, Parker's former colleague at the ad agency in Charlotte, back in the late 80s when they were known as the Wrath Pack, wreaking havoc on the traditional advertising world. When the economy tanked around 1990, all the cutting-edge shit went the way of Men Without Hats. People wanted comfort, and the edgy set were exiled to Advertising Siberia -- doing TV and radio ads for local car or appliance dealerships and churning out print ads for weekly supplements in community newspapers.

Unlike Parker, who served his sentence and moved on to technology PR, Jankowski stuck with the commercial program -- cars, bars, liquor, fashion -- and when the economy roared back by the mid 90s, he was behind the kit again pounding the drums, the coke barely dry in his nostrils. Janko, as he was called by those who didn't despise him (Jankass by those who did), had investment instincts, friends in inside places and a taste for risk, which eventually made him very rich.

"So how exactly do I do that?" asks Parker. "Book myself on Fallon or Colbert? Make a viral video? Engineer a comeback for Paris Hilton? Crash the X Games wearing a sandwich board and riding a BMX"?

"Jesus, and I thought the wise-ass thing was just a phase of yours 20 years ago. You need to *present* yourself. Brand, baby, brand. Get on the speaking circuit. Develop taglines that define what you do in an arresting way. Lean into the authentic thing, because when you're not playing the sarcasm card, you approximate the real deal."

"I've always thought that it's inauthentic to talk about authentic. Isn't authentic something that just is? You think you can manufacture it?"

"You bet your genuine ass, pumpkin. What do you think the Pabst Blue Ribbon people did? All of the sudden that swampy shit is good? You think those bearded dudes in Williamsburg wear re-production gimme hats and Van Heusen shirts because they look good?

"I don't have the personality or inclination for self-promotion. It's just not in my genes."

"What's not in your jeans is the balls to go out there and take some risks. And I'm saying that in the nicest possible way. Because I love you."

"Love like yours could kill a son of a bitch."

An honest F'in bumper

It's an August day in coastal North Carolina that's as rare as a properly cooked tuna steak: 85 degrees with a cooling breeze, not too windy, but strong enough to keep away hungry flies on the beach. It's about an hour before dinner, which Shelly, Uncle Jimmy and Parker already have prepped: crab cakes, sliced tomatoes, potato salad and finely grated cole slaw, light on the mayo, heavier on the white wine vinegar. A pitcher of martinis chills in the freezer: Beefeaters with a whiff of Dolan dry vermouth. Shelly will garnish with a twist of lemon, Uncle Jimmy with a jumbo olive, and Parker with three small pickled onions.

Jimmy and Parker are walking to work up an appetite. Shelly has already biked 10 miles along the beach and did 30 minutes of yoga, so she's good. Jimmy shuffles along the beach kicking sand ahead of him like an eight-year-old.

"Got a pretty hot business idea," Jimmy says.

"Another? Do tell."

"I was strolling around the hood and noticed a car bumper at the edge of the Hooper's lawn a few blocks from the house. Looked brand new; one of those plastic jobbees that are supposed to protect you in a head-on collision. The thing was barely scratched but somehow it had fallen off the car. I don't know if it landed in the Hooper's yard or someone put it there. All I know is that the driver of the car didn't care enough about it to stop and pick it up or to come back searching for it. It was like they threw an empty beer can out the window. So it got me to thinking."

"Uh oh."

"Yeah, I know. But this is no supposition or idle musing, ye of little faith. I'm thinking about whether anyone would pay a premium for an honest-to-god bumper, like the ones they used to make in the 40s and 50s, but highly stylized, even personalized if you

66

really want to pay the big bucks. When I was in Fort Worth last year I saw this place called Rim World, specializing in all kinds of rims for all kinds of vehicles. I'm thinking, why not bumpers? Chrome, titanium, kevlar, silver, jeweled, curvy, reflective, with built-in LED lights if that's your thing."

"I think you're on to something."

"Yes, my young jester, I think I am. My bumpers would take the place of those cheap-ass plastic things. They'd make a statement. An honest fuckin' bumper. Customizable in a thousand different ways; even personalized. They'd be made from kits. You could buy the patterns and raw materials if you have some welding skills or take it to an authorized shop to get it done by a certified technician. There are a bunch of contract manufacturers popping up all over the country that can do customized 3D printing and CNC machining. We could subcontract to them. Or, we could have a central manufacturing facility somewhere in the Midwest and fabricate the bumpers there and ship them whole cloth or in parts for assembly anywhere in the world. It's unique and scalable."

"How much would one pay for this accessory"?

"A lot, and that's part of the marketing. This ain't cheap. It's exclusive. A statement. It would start at $1,500 and go up to $20,000 or more according to level of customization and materials."

"People will pay that"?

"Bet your bippy."

"Wow, Jimmy, you've thought this out."

"Damn straight. Even trademarking a name: 'BumpItGood'."

The lottery host theory

"So where do they find those clothes," asks Parker, pointing to the flat-screen where the mega-jackpot drawing is taking place before the 11 o'clock news.

"What clothes"? answers Shelly.

"The ones the hosts wear for the lottery drawings. They look like leftovers from a 70s cocktail party."

"Aren't you a little young to know that"?

"I watch movies. Plus when I was a kid my mom and dad would go to New Year's Eve parties dressed like that. We'd ask them to bring back hats and noise-makers for us. They'd always do it, but demanded that we don't use the noisemakers until they woke up. That was after I got overzealous at 7 a.m. on New Year's Day and blew one of those paper horns that are rolled up like a hose and then straighten out when you blow them. At the same time, I was twirling around the lever on that thing that makes a loud cranking noise, like a goose in heat. My mother came out of the bedroom and hissed through gritted teeth, 'Stop that. Now.' She was disheveled and my mother was always, at any moment she was awake, sheveled. But, back to the lottery host wardrobe: I have a theory."

"Oh yeah"?

"Yeah. I mean, they probably have wardrobe control over the national telecasts because they are broadcast from a central studio. So they are probably like Motown; they have a wardrobe coordinator, a grooming expert, and a tutor to teach them the enthusiasm and delivery they've all mastered. But here's where it gets interesting: All of the state lottery hosts dress like the national ones and they are scattered out all over the country. So where do they shop?"

"I have no idea, but I'm sure you do."

"I'm thinking there is an exclusive online store for lottery hosts. They have someone who designs all of these dresses and suits and gets them made to order, all the way down to the spangles on the dress and the handkerchief in the dude's sport jacket. Accessories are available too. Rings, tie-tacks, pins, necklaces, bracelets."

"Wigs."

"Yep. And there are videos on how to put together a wardrobe: what to wear in what season. Holiday apparel. Different looks for different areas of the country. How to style your hair for that never flappable look."

"Probably videos on how to get that perkiness into your voice if you don't have it naturally, although that would seem like a prerequisite. But, there might be exercises to maintain it as you grow older and more grizzled. Because life can wear down a lottery host's ass."

"Yeah, especially a lottery host's ass. I mean, I doubt if any of them set out to be a lottery host."

"Yeah, that's not exactly a planned end game."

" 'I want to grow up to be a lottery host' said no kid ever."

Sharing the Love

"That's genius."

"Yeah," says Parker wistfully, shaking his head. "Brian".

"No, I mean the lyrics," says Shelly. "I know Brian had a lot of lyrical partners. Tony Asher, Van Dyke Parks -- they did gorgeous things, totally lock-stepped with what Brian was expressing in the music. But, I'm with Mike -- asshole that he is -- that he was integral to the greatness of many of those hits."

"Yeah"?

"Yeah. Take 'Good Vibrations'. I thought at first it was the height of appropriation that Mike chose that song title for the name of his autobiography. But, those lines he wrote are indelible when teamed with the melody.

'I-I love the colorful clothes she wears
And the way the sunlight plays upon her hair
I hear the sound of a gentle word
On the wind that lifts her perfume through the air'

"Shepherds you into the chorus. He had his own language, and it was perfect for evoking California. I mean, we all have felt 'excitations', but it took Mike to put it in words."

"You might be on to something."

"How about 'Warmth of the Sun'? That song should be a charter member of the American Songbook. Has any pop song ever codified loss like that?

'What good is the dawn
That grows into day
The sunset at night
Or living this way...'

"And the way he came out of the box on 'Do It Again' just grabs you by the back of the neck and pulls you in.

'It's automatic when I talk to old friends
The conversation turns to girls we knew
When their hair was soft and long
And the beach was the place to go.'

"It's not only the lyrics, but his delivery, so matter of fact, so pitch perfect, like speaking a home truth. In tone and pacing, it reminds me of Kerouac's opening to 'Dharma Bums'. You know, 'Hopping a freight out of Los Angeles at high noon one day in late September 1955 I got on a gondola and lay down with my duffel bag under my head and my knees crossed and contemplated the clouds as we rolled north to Santa Barbara'.

"Mike overplays his hand with the lawsuits and the constant pleas for getting credit, but he definitely has a point. Why not put Wilson-Love in the mix with the greatest songwriting teams of our lifetime"?

"Yeah, I guess so. So did you come to this just now"?

"Well, I might have given it a thought or two before this..."

Two lucky guys

"So, how about that email I sent you," asks Jack Benson. Benson is the senior communications manager for Bonsario, a company Parker once worked for and was now engaged with as a freelance writer. Unlike others in his field, Benson was real. He knew the value of honesty within an environment that was as challenged in this regard as a big-stakes poker player. Benson and Parker met once a month or so for drinks and dinner.

"I can't decide if he is slapping someone on the wrist in admonishment or on the ass like an appreciative coach," replied Parker. The "he" is the new CEO, a guy who would take 'two-faced' as a compliment.

"You should have seen the first draft. It would've taken a couple of decades to replant trees on the scorched earth."

"So, what happened between that one and the one you sent"? Parker is simultaneously enthralled with and repulsed by corporate culture, but always curious about it.

"Textbook revision by committee. Every time I tried to put some teeth in it, someone came along and punched them out. Legal committed a red-line massacre. By the fifth draft, I went into 'throw your hands in the air and just don't care' mode."

"I think it would be easy enough to say that stealing proprietary customer data is not in line with company values."

"You'd think so, until the stink of a potential lawsuit seeps like swamp gas into the corporate suite. Then it's 'let the equivocation begin'."

"How do you stand it"? Benson is a few years younger than Parker, in his late 40s, with enough experience to be jaded, but not enough options to go solo or move on to another tech company. Besides, he has good healthcare and an honest-to-god pension, two things for which many managers in today's business environment will put up with heaping piles of steaming shit.

"There's the pay. There's the bennies. There's the fact that no better company is begging for my services. And, there's single malt and wanting to do good by Joan, especially Joan."

"Yeah, you're lucky with that Joan."

"As you are with Shelly."

"Yep. As I am with Shelly."

Things up with which Parker and Shelly will not put

"Oh shit, that's embarrassing."

"What"? asks Shelly. Parker and Shelly are watching Kendrick Lamar, whom they both love, and the live Austin City Limits crowd is getting into it. Predominantly white, they're holding their arms out above chest height at 45-degree angles and thrusting their forearms back towards their bodies as their fingers form gangster digits. Others are doing what used to be the universal slow-down motion: Arms straight above their heads sweeping down to shoulder level in a fanning movement.

"White people posturing".

"Well, it's kind of the universal rapper response. Although come to think of it, I don't see black people doing it very often."

"Unless there are one or two among a crowd of Dukies."

"It could be worse."

"How so"?

"They could be doing the hippy spiritual, wispy dance that chicks who took dance classes in college used to do, even if the song is 'Hot Blooded'."

"Or that lean on the right foot, then lean on the left that men who usually dress in kakis do at weddings."

"We could go on like this for awhile. How about the guitar face that looks like a guy passing a kidney stone."

"Or Andy Murray, the tennis player, flexing his muscles like a boxer at a weigh in...a tennis player for Christ's sake."

"Or the mother dressing like her 14-year-old daughter."

"Or vice versa."

"Or the 40-year-old dude wearing his cap backwards."

"Or anyone wearing his or her cap backwards."

"Sweats on an airplane."

"Bicycle shorts anywhere but on a bicycle."

"Even on a bicycle."

"T-shirts claiming he who dies with the most toys wins."

"Fathers yelling at their sons in public to 'man up'."

"People couching their positions with qualifiers like 'as a radical half-native American feminist and first-in-the-family-college-grad with one blue eye and one grey eye, I think…"

"Muscle guy in the supermarket who flexes while squeezing a cantaloupe."

"Person in a long line at a food truck who's had 15 minutes to memorize the five-item menu while on-line and then has a five-minute conversation with the order taker before making up his mind."

"Parents who use a kid's stroller like a chariot to cut through crowds."

"Shitty tippers."

"People who leave their shopping carts in the middle of the parking lot."

"Double parkers."

"Saying 'no problem' instead of 'thanks'."

"Irish dancers and tenors."

"Artificial sweeteners".

"People who want to change seats on a plane to sit next to their girlfriend, boyfriend, husband, wife, child or co-worker when you're a single person with a clearly superior seat."

"People who say 'I don't disagree' then proceed to disagree."

"A messy hamburger or sub."

"A crab cake that claims to be 'Maryland-Style'."

"Bandwagon fans."

"People who ask questions and are completely uninterested in your answer."

"The Hellman vs. Dukes mayonnaise debate."

"Or any discussion of southern culinary traditions."

"'Best of' lists."

"Any competition or rating list involving the arts."

"Revolutions that aren't even evolutions."

"Nazi comparisons."

"Using 'ain't' to be colloquial."

"Tourists trying to mimic locals."

"Locals hating on tourists who prop up their economy."

"People who say, 'I love me some...'"

"Angular cars."

"Butting into lines."

"Mimes."

"Golf jokes."

"Zealously over-enthusiastic empathy."

"Excessive use of adjectives."

"Men boasting about their grilling skills."

"You know, this could go on for a while."

"Yeah, let's open another bottle of wine."

"People who take solace in wine."

"People who judge people who take solace in wine."

Made in the USA
Columbia, SC
29 June 2021